The House That Went Ker-Splat!
Copyright © 2008 by Bill Myers
Illustrations © 2008 by Andy J. Smith

Requests for information should be addressed to:
Zonderkidz, Grand Rapids, Michigan 49530

Library of Congress Cataloging-in-Publication Data
Myers, Bill, 1953-
The house that went ker-splat! : the parable of the wise and foolish builders / by Bill Myers ; [illustrated by Andy J. Smith].
p. cm.
Summary: In this retelling of the parable of the wise and foolish builders, two wasps take the opposite approach to building their houses, with predictable results.
ISBN-13: 978-0-310-71220-6 (printed hardcover)
ISBN-10: 0-310-71220-3 (printed hardcover)   [1. Insects--Fiction. 2. House construction--Fiction. 3. House built upon a rock (Parable)--Fiction. 4. Parables--Fiction. 5. Christian life--Fiction. 6. Stories in rhyme.] I. Smith, Andy J., 1975- ill. II. Title.
[E]--dc22   PZ8.3.M99534Ho 2008   2007022884

Published in association with the literary agency of Alive Communications, Inc., 7680 Goddard Street #200, Colorado Springs, CO 80920, www.alivecommunications.com

Zonderkidz is a trademark of Zondervan.

Editor: Betsy Flikkema
Art direction & design: Sarah Molegraaf

Printed in China

08 09 10 11 12 • 5 4 3 2 1

THE HOUSE THAT WENT KER-SPLAT!

The Parable of the Wise and Foolish Builders

ZONDERVAN.com/
AUTHORTRACKER
follow your favorite authors

Willie builds homes
like his good buddy Ray.

But the two are as different
as night is from day.

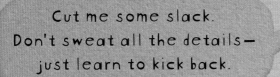

Rules are to follow.

Cut me some slack.
Don't sweat all the details—
just learn to kick back.

Their boss shows them blueprints.

These plans you must follow.

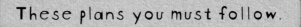

I'll study in detail.

Yeah, maybe tomorrow.

They each find locations.

Next come plumbers and framers
and electricians too.

Willie buys wood from drivers he trusts.

But Ray hires termites.

All **I've** got is sawdust!

And finally the roof...
Lay those tiles nice and tight.
A roof? We don't need one.
This way there's more light!

At last they are finished.
Their deadlines are met.

DANGER
NO BUILD ZONE

Don't tell me that's thunder.

Hey, boss!
I'm all wet.

The storm grows more fierce
as the wind starts to howl.
Ray's walls begin falling.

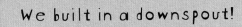

And then just like that—
as in one second flat—
the house is washed out
with a new sound...

KER-SPLAT!

DANGER
No BUILD
ZONE

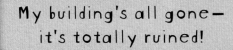

And so as they haul
Ray off to do time,
Willie's house stays intact.

This one looks fine.

BLOK-O

And what is the difference
between these two friends?
I follow what's written.
I thought rules
were to bend.

It's much like our life:
God gives us his plan.
We can build upon it...
or upon shifting sand.

One may be harder,
but it's always the best...

'cause I'll always love you
and see that you're blessed.